90005169

THE LIMA BEAN MONSTER

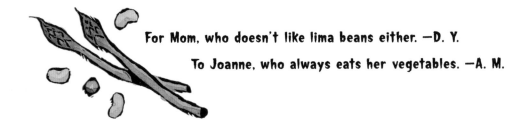

For Mom, who doesn't like lima beans either. —D. Y.

To Joanne, who always eats her vegetables. —A. M.

First published in the United States of America in 2001
by Walker Publishing Company, Inc.

Published simultaneously in Canada by Fitzhenry and Whiteside, Markham, Ontario L3R 4T8

Library of Congress Cataloging-in-Publication Data

Yaccarino, Dan.
    The lima bean monster / Dan Yaccarino ; illustrations by Adam McCauley.
        p. cm.
    Summary: After Sammy's dumping of the lima beans he does not want to eat starts a neighborhood
trend to put rejected vegetables in a hole on a vacant lot, a terrible lima bean monster rises to
terrorize the town.
ISBN 0-8027-8776-2 -- ISBN 0-8027-8777-0
[1. Lima bean--Fiction. 2. Food habits--Fiction. 3. Monsters--Fiction.] I. McCauley, Adam, ill. II. Title.

PZ7.Y125 Li 2001
[E--dc21   2001026011

The artist used mixed media on watercolor paper to create the illustrations for this book.

Book design by Cynthia Wigginton

Printed in Hong Kong

10 9 8 7 6 5 4 3 2 1

THE LIMA BEAN MONSTER

Dan Yaccarino

Illustrations by Adam McCauley

Walker & Company
New York

Sammy hated lima beans. He hated them so much
that he hadn't eaten a single one in his whole life.

His Mom tried a MILLION
different ways to make them.

Lima bean SOUP,
lima bean CASSEROLE,

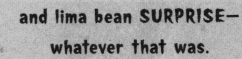

and lima bean SURPRISE—
whatever that was.

One night she gave up and made no attempt to hide them at all, just plain old lima beans. That was the worst. Sammy stared down at them sitting there on his plate and they stared right back.

"Oh, for heaven's sake," said Mom. "Just eat them. They're good for you."

Each night Sammy tried a new way to get rid of those crummy lima beans. He hid them underneath the mashed potatoes or stuffed them into his napkin. Once he tried feeding them to his dog, but Blackie was too smart for that.

Then he had a brilliant idea. While Mom wasn't looking, Sammy pretended to eat the beans while quickly stuffing them in his sock.

"Mmmmmmm, that was just swell, Mom," said Sammy. "Gee whiz, those beans must be good for me! I feel like going outside to play!"

Before he was excused from the table, a skeptical Mom checked all the usual places for Sammy's unwanted lima beans, but they were nowhere to be found.

Sammy ran out the back door and down the street
with a sock full of hot, squishy beans. When he got to the
vacant lot at the end of his block he dug a hole. Sammy
tossed the beans in and covered them with dirt.

"Heh, heh, heh," snickered Sammy. "I'll never have to eat
lima beans as long as I live!"

Well, you'll never guess what Mom made the next night—that's right—more lima beans!

"Since you enjoyed them so much last night, I decided to make them again!" Mom said happily.

Let Mom pile on as many lima beans as she wanted, Sammy had a surefire way of getting rid of them!

This time, as Sammy threw the beans into the hole in the vacant lot, his friend Chester walked by.

"What'cha doin', Sammy?" asked Chester.

Sammy explained his brilliant method of disposing of unwanted vegetables. Chester agreed: It was brilliant! The next night Chester was tossing his lima beans into the hole right along with Sammy's.

News traveled fast, and soon all the kids in the neighborhood were throwing their brussels sprouts, parsnips, and lima beans down into the hole. Before long they started bringing other things they didn't like. Ugly birthday sweaters, failed spelling tests, tap shoes, and even an accordion. Sammy had to draw the line when Chester tried to throw his baby brother in.

One night there was a huge storm. Snug and warm in his bed, Sammy listened to the thunder grumble and watched the lightning streak across the sky. It struck everything it could find: tall trees, telephone poles, and even the church steeple.

By this time, that little mound of dirt in the vacant lot had grown big and tall. The lightning decided to strike that, too. Not once, but twice!

All through the night the mound glowed and glowed and grew and grew until, all of a sudden, the ground burst open and out crawled a huge, ugly, scary creature! It was as tall as a tree and it stank of lima beans and sweaty socks! Yuck!

The monster stomped through the neighborhood, tossing around cars and stepping on houses. People screamed and ran in all directions to get away from the horrible stinky monster.

"RRRRRRROOOOOAAAAARRRRR!" it roared as it almost stepped on Chester. "Me want some HUMAN beans!"

"Help!" cried Chester. "Somebody save us!"

At that moment, Sammy was too busy holding his nose and running in the other direction to hear Chester. The rampaging monster spotted Sammy and scooped him up in his massive paw. His smelly breath almost made Sammy faint.

"Me eat some human beans!" he bellowed.

"Wait!" cried Sammy. "Don't eat me! I-I'm too small! Wouldn't you like to eat someone bigger?"

After examining him thoroughly, the Lima Bean Monster agreed. The ever-helpful Sammy pointed out his science teacher making a fast getaway down Elm Street. "Now there's a meal!" Sammy said.

The monster dropped Sammy, roared down Elm Street, and scooped up Sammy's science teacher. "Eat LOTS of big human beans!" he growled, and proceeded to grab every single grown-up in the neighborhood.

"Help!" they pleaded.

"We're doomed!" hollered Chester's dad.

"What a way to go!" wailed the science teacher.

"Do something, Sammy!" cried Sammy's mom.

"Chester! I've got an idea!" Sammy exclaimed. "First, we've got to round up every kid we know!"

Sammy and Chester got all the kids together and they quickly formed a circle around the giant.

The Lima Bean Monster looked down at them and laughed, "Me come back when you little sprouts are bigger! Ha! Ha! Ha!!"

He opened wide and prepared to drop Chester's dad into his gaping gullet just as Sammy cried out, "Okay, everybody, there's only one way out....Eat your vegetables!"

The monster howled as hundreds of tiny little teeth nibbled at his feet, chomped on his kneecaps, and chewed his arms until there was nothing left of him at all, except for half of an ugly birthday sweater.

When it was over, everyone cried, "Hooray for Sammy!" They carried him up and down the street on their shoulders.

That night, as Sammy's mom tucked him in, he asked, "You know what, Mom?"

"What's that, dear?" asked Mom.

Sammy thought for a moment and said, "Lima beans aren't so bad after all."

"Really," said Mom. "How do you feel about turnips?"

"Don't push your luck, Mom."

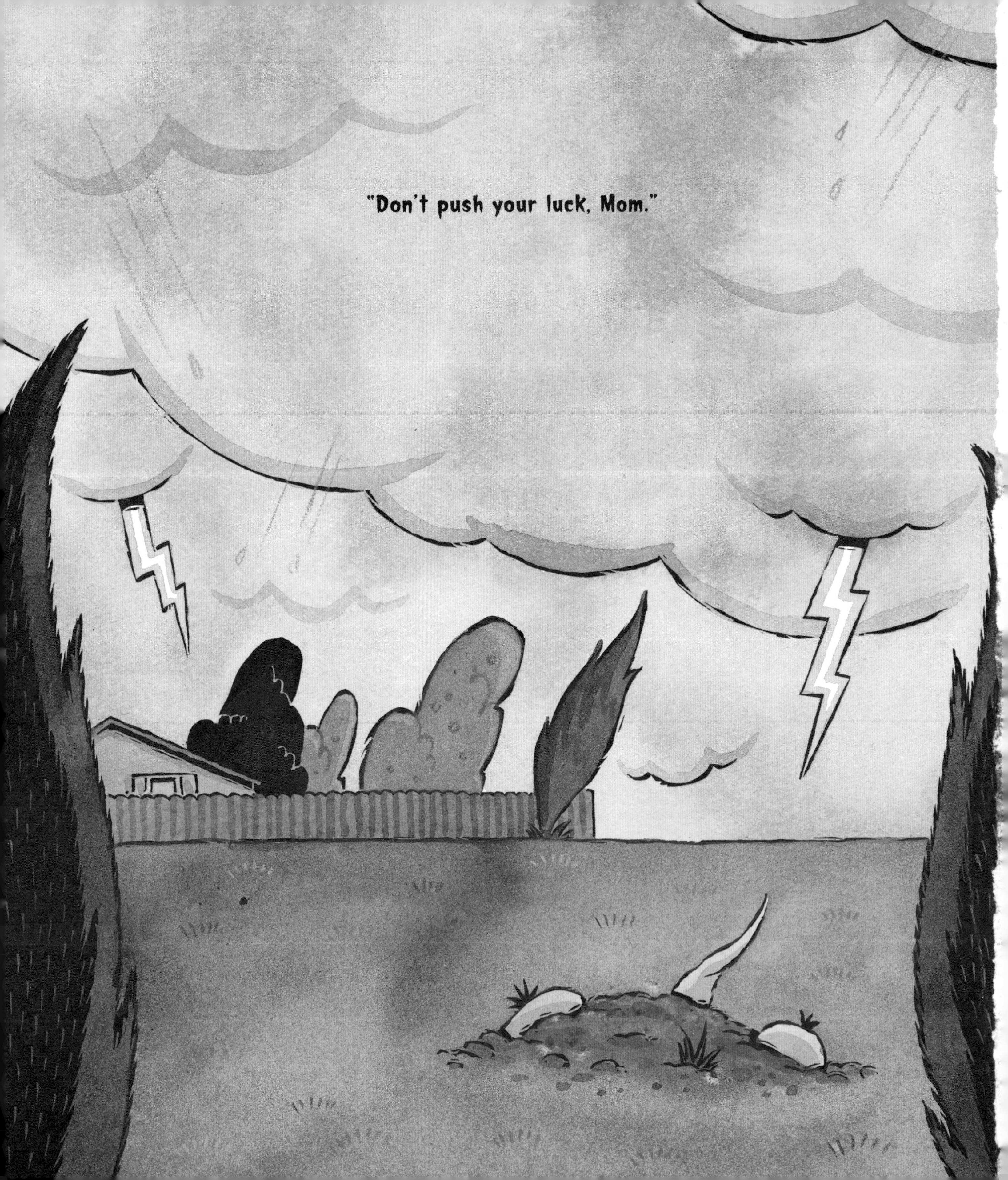